THE SEALS
ON THE BUS

by LENNY HORT

BUS STOP

Come to the
☆BIG PARTY☆
everyone invited!

illustrated by

G. BRIAN KARAS

Henry Holt and Company · New York

Go out on the Town
on the
Z1

Henry Holt and Company, LLC
Publishers since 1866
115 West 18th Street, New York, New York 10011

Henry Holt and Company is a registered trademark of Henry Holt and Company, LLC
Text copyright © 2000 by Lenny Hort. Illustrations copyright © 2000 by G. Brian Karas.
All rights reserved. Published in Canada by Fitzhenry & Whiteside Ltd.,
195 Allstate Parkway, Markham, Ontario L3R 4T8.

Library of Congress Cataloging-in-Publication Data
Hort, Lenny. The seals on the bus / by Lenny Hort; illustrated by G. Brian Karas.
Summary: Different animals—including seals, tigers, geese, rabbits, monkeys, and
more—make their own sounds as they ride all around town on a bus.
1. Children's songs—Texts. [1. Animal sounds—Songs and music. 2. Buses—
Songs and music. 3. Songs.] I. Karas, G. Brian, ill. II. Title.
PZ8.3.H7875 Se   2000   782.42164'0268—dc21   [E]   99-033612

The artist used gouache, acrylic medium, pencil, and cut paper to create
the illustrations for this book.

ISBN 0-8050-5952-0 / First Edition—2000 / Designed by Donna Mark
Printed in the United States of America on acid-free paper. ∞
10 9 8 7 6 5 4 3 2

For Irene, all around the town

—L. C. H.

For Benjamin and Samuel

—G. B. K.

The seals on the bus go

ERRP, ERRP, ERRP,

ERRP, ERRP, ERRP,

ERRP, ERRP, ERRP.

The seals on the bus go
ERRP, ERRP, ERRP,

All around the town.

The tiger on the bus goes **ROAR, ROAR, ROAR,**

ROAR,
ROAR,
ROAR,
ROAR,
ROAR,
ROAR,
ROAR.

The tiger on the bus goes
ROAR, ROAR, ROAR,

All around the town.

The geese on the bus go

The geese on the bus go
HONK, HONK, HONK,

All around the town.

The rabbits on the bus go
UP AND **DOWN,**
UP AND **DOWN,**
UP AND **DOWN.**

The rabbits on the bus go
UP AND **DOWN**,

All around the town.

The monkeys on the bus go

The monkeys on the bus go
EEEEH, EEEEH, EEEEH,

Town
Z1

All around the town.

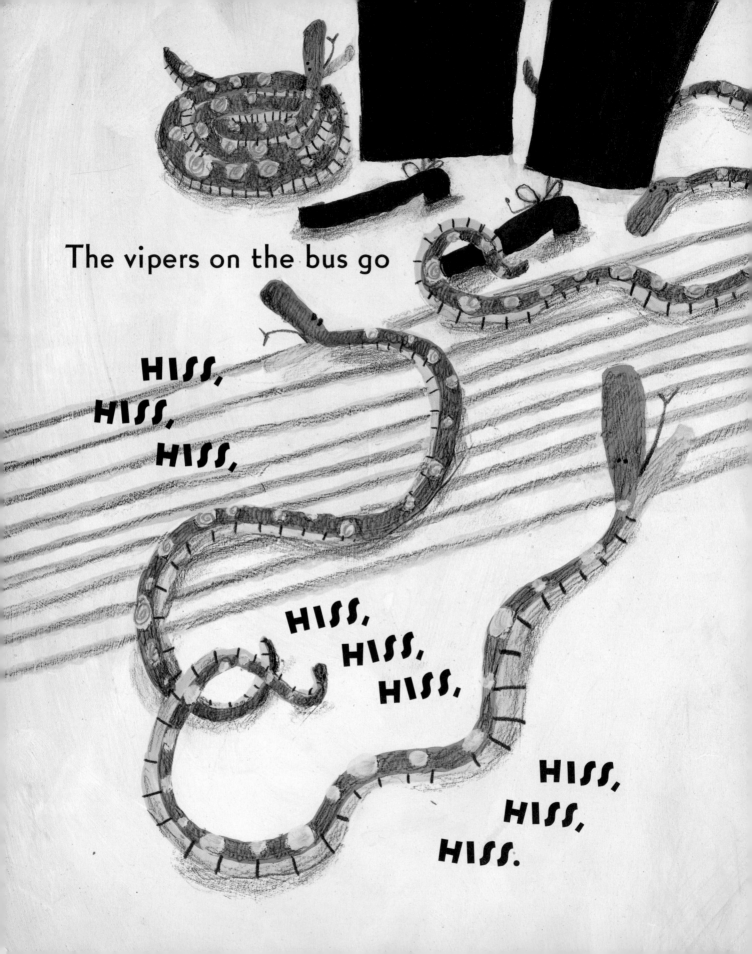

The vipers on the bus go

HISS,
HISS,
HISS,

HISS,
HISS,
HISS,

HISS,
HISS,
HISS.

The vipers on the bus go
HISS, HISS, HISS,

All around the town.

The sheep on the bus go

BAAH,
BAAH,
BAAH,

BAAH,
BAAH,
BAAH,

The sheep on the bus go
BAAH, BAAH, BAAH,

All around the town.

The skunks on the bus go
SSSSS,
SSSSS,
SSSSS,

SSSSS,
SSSSS,
SSSSS,

SSSSS,
SSSSS,
SSSSS.

The skunks on the bus go
sssss, sssss, sssss,

All around the town.

Go Out
on th

And the people on the bus go

The people on the bus go
HELP, HELP, HELP!

All around the town.